Saddle the Sun

To Lois Adella Fuller Taylor,
my meemaw and the best bedtime storytelling grandma ever —T.H.

By Trish Holland
Illustrated by Ben Mantle

A GOLDEN BOOK • NEW YORK

Text copyright © 2023 by Trish Holland
Cover and interior illustrations copyright © 2023 by Ben Mantle
All rights reserved. Published in the United States by Golden Books, an imprint of
Random House Children's Books, a division of Penguin Random House LLC, 1745 Broadway,
New York, NY 10019. Golden Books, A Golden Book, A Little Golden Book, the G colophon,
and the distinctive gold spine are registered trademarks of Penguin Random House LLC.
rhcbooks.com
Educators and librarians, for a variety of teaching tools, visit us at RHTeachersLibrarians.com
Library of Congress Control Number: 2022931981
ISBN 978-0-593-30655-0 (trade) — ISBN 978-0-593-30656-7 (ebook)
Printed in the United States of America
10 9 8 7 6 5 4 3 2 1

Hey! I'm Little Tex.

And I'm Rio Rosie.
It's time to giddyup.
There's no time to mosey.

We jam on our hats,
Tug boots on our feet.
But where is our breakfa[s]
Fresh eggs we can eat?

The coop's full of chickens,
But they will not lay
Till light brands the sky
At the dawn of the day.

So we saddle the sun
And ride high in the sky.
But the heat beating down
Bakes the land very dry.

So we round up some rain clouds
To water the crop.
But once it gets started,
The rain just won't stop.

So we scoop a deep hole
For the rain and the mud.

But the lake fills up quick,
And it's threatening to flood.

So we hog-tie the storm clouds
And drag them away.

But the thunder's last BOOM
Spooks the longhorns astray.

Now our tummies are rumbling,
And lunchtime has passed.
But our home is in danger.
We've got to move fast!

So we lift up the ranch house
Above the stampede.
But the herd keeps on running,
'Cause cows cannot read.

They dash past the bunkhouse,
The barn, and a field.

They're tough and they're stubborn.
Those dogies won't yield.

Oh, no—there's a cliff!
So on horses we hop.

We fly to the edge,
Turn around, and yell

STOP!

The cows look surprised,
But they slam on the brakes.

Dust shoots to the sky.
The ground trembles and shakes.

We can't see a thing
Through the huge cloud of dirt.

But when it all settles—
No creatures are hurt.

We've rescued the longhorns.
There's no more to fear.
The chuck wagon's coming!
Our vittles are here!

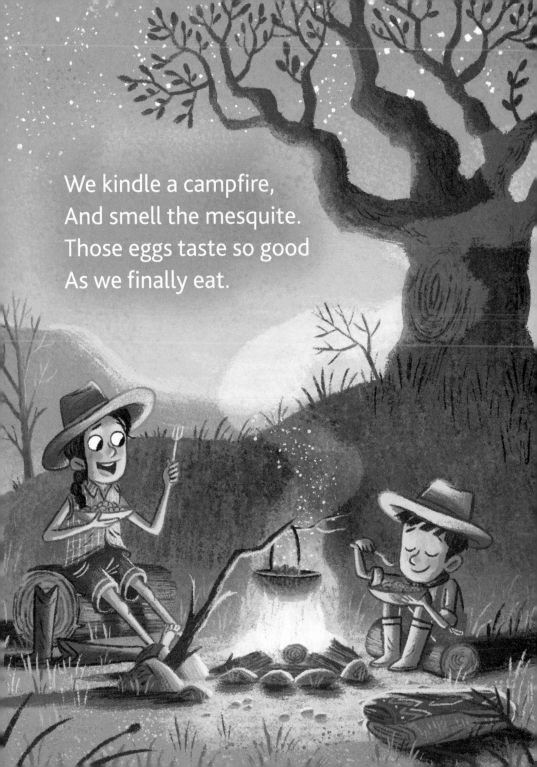

We kindle a campfire,
And smell the mesquite.
Those eggs taste so good
As we finally eat.

We shake out our bedrolls.
The sun will set soon.
We sing and then sleep
By the light of the moon.